THE BIG COMFY COUCH ™

Hello
Molly!

Written by **Cheryl Wagner**

Illustrated by **Cheryl Roberts**

TIME LIFE Kids ™

ALEXANDRIA,
VIRGINIA

Once upon a couch, a Big Comfy
Couch, there lived a little
clown named Loonette.
Loonette was a busy,
bouncy clown, full of
imagination. She loved
to play on her couch.
She had lots of toys and
books. But she had no one
to play with.

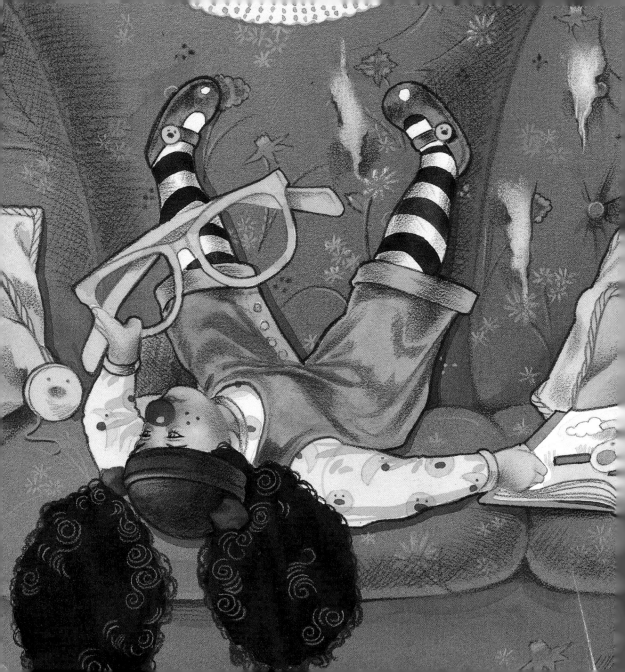

Loonette loved games.
But it's hard to play
tag, or hide and
seek, or peek-a-boo
all by yourself.
The little clown
especially loved to put
on her big glasses
and read a story out
loud. But she had no
one to show the
pictures to.

Loonette tried playing outside, but
sitting on a seesaw all by herself
wasn't much fun either.

She felt lonely. She needed
something. But she didn't know
what that something might be.

Then, as Loonette looked
around for a new game to play,
she saw a parachute floating
down from the sky, with
somebody hanging from it.

"Auntie Macassar!" she
called. "Is that you?"

Auntie Macassar, the world-traveling clown, landed right on the seesaw.

"What's the matter, Loonette?" she asked. "You look a little sad."

"There's nothing fun to do, and nobody to play with," Loonette said. "I need something—but I don't know what!"

"I have an idea, Loonette," Auntie Macassar said. "Why don't we go in to Clowntown for a special treat? We can think about what you need on the way."

"Oh, good!" the little clown said, turning a cartwheel. "Do you think we could go to the Donut Shop? Please?"

So off they went.

But on their way to the Donut Shop, they came across the biggest yard sale Loonette had ever seen.

There were stuffed animals and bowling balls, skis and magic wands, paintbrushes and goofy clown clothes. It had everything a clown could want!

Too noisy

Too fancy!

Too big!

Maybe a new toy will make me happy, Loonette thought. She looked and looked.

"Too big."

"Too noisy."

"Too fancy."

Nothing seemed exactly right. "I still don't know what I'm looking for," Loonette said. "Maybe we should just go on to the Donut Shop."

Just then she saw a barrel in a corner of the yard. On it was a sign that said: FREE TO A GOOD HOME.

Loonette walked over to the barrel. She couldn't believe her eyes—a donut!

"Who is thinking of a donut?" the little clown wondered as she looked inside.

Loonette reached into the barrel and pulled out the most wonderful little doll! Right away she knew she had found someone special.

"Hello," she said. "My name is Loonette the clown. So you like donuts too? What else makes you happy? Do you like storybooks? I have lots of stories at home that we could read together. Would you like to come home with me?"

Auntie Macassar joined them. "Did you find a toy, Loonette?"

"Better than a toy!" Loonette said. "I've found someone I can play with. Someone who likes the same things I do."

"Then you've found a friend!" said Auntie Macassar with a smile.

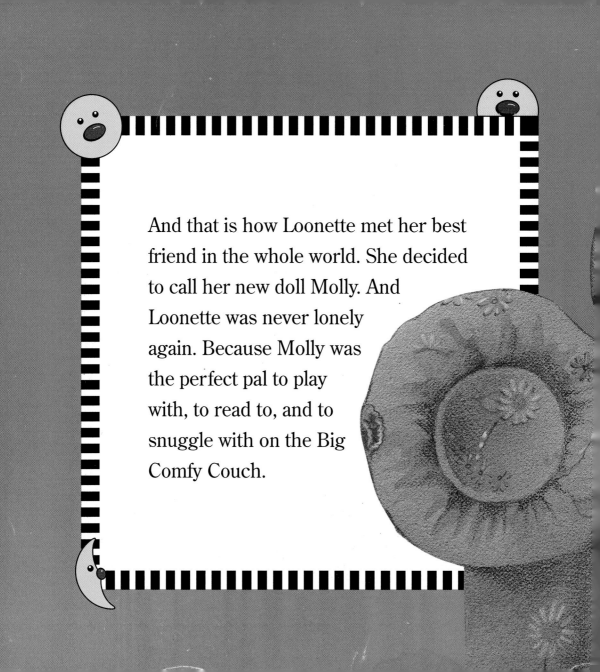

And that is how Loonette met her best friend in the whole world. She decided to call her new doll Molly. And Loonette was never lonely again. Because Molly was the perfect pal to play with, to read to, and to snuggle with on the Big Comfy Couch.